ISBN: 978-1-939484-48-2

Photography Dale Diessner & Helen Diessner

Cover by Stephen R Walker
SRWALKERDESIGNS.COM

Crowe Press

I0537440

GEORGE HAINT

An unusual ghost story by Helen Diessner
with
Marta Moran Bishop.

FORWARD

Helen Diessner began this story in 2012. We discussed it and talked about how she wanted it to end.

I was with her in Carson City Nevada in September of 2021 when she passed away, and promised I'd finish her story and get it published.

My hope is the little bits I added would have been what she wanted.

Helen was my best friend as well as my sister, and I inherited this story along with a few other mementos. I miss her still.

The shack pictured on the cover is one she took near her apartment in the Gold-Hill area of Virginia City. She loved to watch the wild horses come down from the hills and the birds at the feeders on her deck.

After her husband passed away Helen worked at Way it was Museum for a period. Visited friends at some of the local historical saloons and watched the Chicago Cubs on both the TV and internet (when they were not shown locally.)

I don't recall there being anything about the Virginia City area that Helen didn't love, except perhaps living so far away from her daughters and siblings.

Along with her love of reading, the Chicago Cubs, football and her cat Toby, Helen loved her family, friends, politics and life.

Marta Moran Bishop

From the original portion of Helen's manuscript.

To Ken Bishop who gave me the inspiration for the title character and to Marta Moran Bishop and Ken Bishop whose love, support, encouragement, and unwavering belief in me kept the thought alive and helped me finish it.

CHAPTER ONE

George woke while it was still dark outside. Since Mary had died it seemed the days were turned upside down. The day became night, and night day.

Lying awake in bed, thinking about how much he missed her, wondering *will I ever wake without my first thoughts being of Mary*? Still longing for her warmth as he lay in bed, and oh, how he missed waking up to the aroma of coffee brewing and bacon sizzling in the frying pan. *Mary had died so many years ago*. He thought. "One would think I'd have put her memory farther back into the recesses of my mind, instead I still wake expecting to see her."

George had never owned a bathrobe, but on this morning, he wished he had one, he thought. Slowly swinging his legs off the bed and slipping his feet into the mules on the floor. "This little house is so cold I feel the need to wrap myself in one of these blankets." Shuffling across the room and sitting at the small table envisioning having his morning coffee with Mary as they had done while she had been alive. It was a ritual he had always enjoyed before going to work at the Yellow Clydeet mine.

Mining was backbreaking and exhausting work, but thoughts of coming home to Mary always got him through the day. But now, there was no Mary to come home to, just an empty house that had fallen into such disarray over the years that it was nothing more than a shack.

George and Mary had built the little house themselves, and although it was only a one-room cottage, Mary had always made it feel more like a palace. She had made the place cozy and comfortable. On the windows still hung the shreds of the once pink and white cotton curtains she had made by hand but were now torn and dirty. The floor that once shone so brightly from the waxing and buffing his wife did religiously once a week, was now so dirty and splintered it appeared as though it had not been swept in a hundred years. The wallpaper with the tiny roses had faded and peeled from the walls. The windows had long ago been broken by vandals and yet George seemed not to notice. When it got cold or the snow came in, he just wrapped himself up in more blankets, just as he'd always done, though he didn't really feel the cold.

He knew he had given up living since he lost Mary, but death had not come for him. What he did know, however, was he had stopped caring about anything except Mary. There were times he felt like she was still with him. He'd sit for hours talking to her and most of the time, he was sure she responded to him.

In the center of the room was a large pot-bellied iron stove which served both for cooking and heating. The bed and dresser were on the south side of the room. Near the bedroom area was a small brocade-covered settee, now threadbare and so dusty that George no longer used it. Even in his sleep, it haunted him with the fond memories of the days he and Mary had sat talking; she in the old rocker and him on the settee. The rocker had aged so rapidly since his wife's death, it was almost as though she had been its life source and without her, it was dying like the rest of the house.

They met while they were still in their teens; she was fifteen and he, seventeen. For George, it had been love at first sight, and they married within weeks of their first date in the Lutheran church in Germantown, Pennsylvania. Mary's parents were opposed to the marriage, wishing she would wed someone with better financial prospects, but when she had threatened to elope with George, they conceded the battle and allowed the wedding to take place.

George got employment almost immediately at the coal mine where his father worked. He hated it, but it supported them. The hours were long, the wages low and the conditions dangerous.

When news of the gold discovery at Sutter's Mill reached Germantown, George decided to take Mary and head to California. Although it would take them several years to save enough money for the trip, George was sure there would be a better fortune for them in the west.

He and Mary packed as many of their belongings as they could on a wagon and used the last of his wages to purchase another mule.

In the April of 1853, they set off for California with dreams of wealth and better times to fuel them. If they'd realized how difficult and long the journey would be, they might have thought better of making the trip west, but they were still young, and filled with optimism.

In the evenings they would rest the mules and build a campfire and Mary would fix salt pork and beans for supper. They sat for hours talking about their plans when they reached California. George was sure they would find plenty of riches and even though Mary wasn't sure it was possible, she clung to his belief and seldom complained about the hard ground, rain, smoke from the campfire, or privations they went through. The dream made it easier to get up each morning and begin the journey onward.

Just before they reached Colorado, they met up with three families who were making the California trip and decided that there would be more safety in joining them. Across the plains and into the mountains they trekked, each family helping the other over the steep and forbidding passes. At nightfall, they would get together and share meals, laughter, and their dreams.

The women would prepare coffee and bread for breakfast while the men hooked up the team. They plodded along through the sweltering heat, weathered the pouring rain, and slept through the cold nights. The days turned to weeks, the weeks into months.

It was October 1853, when George and his party reached an area in the Utah Territory known as "Devil's Gate." They discovered a small settlement consisting of shacks and miners who informed the wagon party that gold had been discovered – gold enough for them all to become rich. George, Mary, and the others in their party sat down to discuss whether they should stay and mine the area with the others or continue onward to California. Since it was already late in October and would possibly have to put the balance of their trip on hold until spring, they all agreed to stay in Devil's Gate and try to make their fortunes.

The Utah Territory was still mostly an unchartered area and had few trees suitable for building a home.

Devil's Gate, sat in a canyon surrounded by mountains. Winds came howling through the mountains almost daily and were frequently strong enough to knock a man out of his boots! There were Indians in the area who called themselves Piutes, but the local citizenry informed George that these people had been peaceful enough and should result in no threat to any of them.

George set out to find whatever he could in the manner of wood in which he might build a cabin for Mary and him. He located a few poplar trees, cut them down, and with his wagon and mule, brought them to a location approximately two miles up the mountain to a location that had no mining or construction and immediately set to building a small shelter. In a matter of weeks, the building was done, and they moved their meager belongings from the wagon into the shack. Behind the house, he fenced off a small area for the mule and Mary put herself to making the shack a home.

The pair removed the table, settee, and rocker from the wagon. George put together a bed from poplar and placed their cotton-stuffed mattress between the supports. The dishes sat in their packing awaiting the construction of shelves. The next concern would be a stove for heating and cooking, but that would have to wait until they replenished their funds. George would have to find gold or work and needed to do it quickly before winter set in.

Often in the evenings he sat around the campfire of one of his fellow miners and listen to stories of the gold discoveries in Devil's Gate or farther north up the mountains. A few of his friends had discovered gold, but generally no more than a few small nuggets they panned from the creek which ran through the canyon.

George sat silently at the small wooden table, reminiscing and staring out the window. He had no ambition to even prepare himself a cup of coffee. It seemed like forever since he had eaten anything. He just wasn't hungry. His lack of meals didn't appear to be hurting him. His clothes still fit properly so he wasn't losing weight. He would fix himself something later. George didn't voice it aloud, but he knew he was a broken man and wondered how long before he'd be following Mary in death.

They hadn't had children. Not that they didn't want them, but children just never came. They didn't care too much, because they had each other and the hours, days, and years they spent together were filled with laughter and love and the kind of friendship that only comes with years of closeness and sharing.

But over the years, after Mary died George became aware he was becoming bitter and angry which he attributed to his loneliness for companionship. *Somehow it feels that the anger came before Mary's death. But I don't know why.* George thought.

Of course, he still had the fellows he worked with at the mine for company, but even they seemed distant and unresponsive. It was just a job now, and he put in his time and seldom spoke to anyone. He felt he was just putting in this time until he joined Mary. It just wasn't fair that he was so alone while all his co-workers had people with whom they could share the good times, laughing and drinking with the girls from D Street, or playing poker, faro, or other games of chance at the local taverns.

Before Mary had passed, George found gold and silver, just as many others did. Fantastic gold and silver deposits were found just north of Devil's Gate and an entire town had grown around them.

An old miner nicknamed, "Old Virginny," had been responsible for the naming of the area, Virginia City, on an evening when he had been quite inebriated and broken his whiskey bottle. George remembered "Old Virginny" lamenting over the broken bottle losing its content and being a good-natured man, simply turned the loss into a joke, saying, "I now Christen this place as Virginia." Mines grew rapidly in the area. Everyone had plenty of money. People purchased goods or good times with gold nuggets, raw silver, or shares in mining operations. Virginia City was the richest city in the west!

Virginia City was the richest city in the world! The entire area which included, Gold Hill, Silver City, and Virginia City became known as the "Comstock Lode." It was given its name by a fellow named

Henry P.T. Comstock who had bluffed his way into a goldmine stake.

George and Mary moved to one of the hotels in the town and frequented some of the fine dining establishments and occasionally even managed an evening at Piper's Opera House. Those were wonderful, exciting days!

"Mary, why did you need to spoil everything by complaining when I came home smelling of cheap perfume and whiskey.' George said looking at the rocking chair. 'It wasn't as if you were neglected. I mean a man needs to sow some of the wild oats, even if he does it when he is older."

Except for those few times that Mary complained they had been happy and imagined those days would never end.

But then, in 1864, Mary had become ill and died within days. Nothing would ever be good again. All around him people still worked and laughed and played. The world went on for everyone except George. And George hated the world and everyone in it. Somehow, he had to make them understand. They must know how he was suffering. He would make them feel his anger, his loss, and his hurt.

CHAPTER TWO

George watched from the shadows behind one of the "cribs" on D Street. Myron Givins was inside the house with one of the girls who worked for Julia Boulette. Julia was the most famous madam in Virginia City, for that matter, possibly the most famous in the west.

Myron fancied himself in love. He was so smitten with Sylvia; he had spent almost every dollar he earned and as much spare time as he could with her. He was sure that soon he would be able to convince her to marry him. Myron hoped to take her to California with him for a fresh start, and to that end, was selling his mining shares and quietly secreting money for a nest egg. He and Sylvia had begun talking about a future, although she had made no commitment to marriage, Myron was positive he could convince her to be his wife.

As George listened to the laughter and raucous music coming from the D Street crib, he patiently awaited Myron's exit. Myron must suffer and feel the pain that he felt. Myron had ignored George whenever he tried to speak with him about Mary's passing. If Myron would have shown some sympathy, it would not have come to this, so it wasn't George's fault that Myron must be punished. It was Myron's fault. And he shouldn't be happy while George suffered.

About 11:15, Myron exited Sylvia's crib, telling her he would return shortly with some more champagne, and happily winded his way up the hill to C Street, whistling as he walked. Myron appeared too happy for George to tolerate, but he won't be for long, he thought.

Once George was sure that Myron was out of sight, he went to Sylvia's door and tapped gently. Sylvia answered the door with a smile, saying "did you forget something?" Apparently, she thought I was Myron. I quickly shoved Sylvia backward into the room and closed the door. Before she had an opportunity to scream, I slammed my fist into her face, knocking her unconscious. I then locked the door and turned off all the lights.

I remember dragging Sylvia to the settee, tying her securely with the drapery cords, placing a gag in her mouth. Then reviving her by pouring water on her face. When she became conscious, I began my task. She could not see me in the darkness, but I had no problem seeing her. I took my knife and slowly carved away at her face. As the blood began flowing, I felt so alive! I hadn't felt this alive since Mary died. I sliced her gown and corset revealing her ample breasts and slowly plunged the knife between them. I could see a silent scream in her face; a face which now was frozen in death. Now all I had to do was to wait. I found a spot in the shadows outside her door and watched the street for Myron. It was only a few minutes when I spotted him, still whistling, walking down the street carrying a bottle of champagne.

When Myron reached the door, he found it opened and the lights off. He lit the lamp near the door and called "Sylvia, I'm back." Receiving no answer, his eyes scanned the room to the settee and immediately saw Sylvia, in a pool of blood with her face frozen in terror and no signs of life. Myron screamed. He screamed again and then ran. Myron knew someone would accuse him of Sylvia's death since just about everyone in town knew he visited her nightly.

The following morning, news of Sylvia's sadistic murder was talked about throughout the Comstock and had reached the ears of Sheriff, Jerry Anton, who immediately began questioning suspects. Of course, the main suspect was Myron Givens, and he could not be found.
George wondered if Myron was feeling the same kind of loss and pain that he felt. But George already knew the answer to that question. He

knew the answer when he had seen the expression on Myron's face. And George felt good. He felt alive. Some of the pain and anger was gone, at least for now.

CHAPTER THREE

Yet it came back, again and again, returning and each time George's only relief came from carving up another whore.

Where was I? George thought. *Oh yes, thinking about the first one. Or was it really the first, he wondered again.* Something just didn't sit right in his mind about it being the first.

"I need another fix he said aloud.' Looking around the shack again. 'Why ever did Mary and I move back here? We had such a lovely place in the Gold-Hill area of Virginia City. Did we move back here together?' He questioned aloud for the umpteenth time. 'I just don't remember. Why don't I remember? I seem to have such gaps in my memory, and I DO NOT LIKE IT." He yelled at the empty chair.

But the chair didn't answer, it never did no matter how long George stared at it.

Moving his gaze to the open window, George said. "Why doesn't anyone come to visit, or check on me anymore? It's as if I'm invisible to them. I HATE THAT. He yelled. 'I don't like being invisible. I'll make them see me. I'll make them remember

GEORGE HAINT. My name will go down in history." Just then he heard voices outside.

"We can be alone in that shack, Elizabet."

"It scares me, I heard it was haunted, Clyde."

"I don't believe in haints, do you? I mean seriously we can get in out of the cold night and be alone for a while in there."

"What's a haint?"

"It's an old word for ghost or evil spirit in the south Elizabet."

"I like that word, but I'm not sure about going in there, Clyde. It looks spooky to me."

George peered out the window at the young pair. *I'll just tell them to get lost if they come in here.* He thought watching the boy put his arm around the blonde girl. *What a pretty thing she is, it might be fun watching them instead of ordering them out.*

He watched Clyde whispering in her ear, slowly trailing his fingers down her face, across her full lips, and finally kissing her.

George Haint

Yes, I'll watch for a bit. But where to hide? It's dark in here, perhaps if I just stand in the shadows, they won't see me until it's too late. George thought slithering into the darkest corner of the room.

Opening the creaky door, Clyde glanced around pulling Elizabet in behind them. "It's pretty dusty in here, but we can shake out the bedding."

Squinting up her pretty nose, Elizabet said. "Clyde it's creepy."

Turning to her he pulled her into his arms again, stroking her hair, back and teasing her with his kisses, until she was breathless, and stopped thinking, he picked her up carrying her to the bed.

They couldn't get enough of each other, as they pulled their clothes off until skin met skin, and they fell to the bed.

A smile spread across George's face. *This is going to be fun.* He thought. *When they are done, that is when I will show myself.* His hand grabbed the ax sitting in the corner next to him.

Oblivious to anything but each other, breathing heavily, Clyde and Elizabet slowly made love.

Their hands caressing each other nothing else existed for either of them but the moment and the feel of each other.

"I love you, Elizabet.' Clyde said stroking her face, his lips finding her swollen mouth again. 'I didn't hurt you, did I?"

"Only for a minute Clyde. Then it was glorious." She said, her mouth still touching his.

"Do you love me, Elizabet?"

"God yes.' She said her hand moving down his chest caressing lower and lower. 'Do you want more too Clyde?"

"YES!" He said.

CHAPTER FOUR

Leering at them, with a smile on his face. George thought. *This is going to be better than any of the others.*

Suddenly George saw Mary. She was standing right in front of him. "NO GEORGE, NOT THIS TIME." She yelled. YOU WILL LEAVE THEM ALONE. WHAT KIND OF MONSTER HAVE YOU BECOME? Her anger allowed her to finally find her voice.

"You're dead Mary."

"Yes, I am and so are you. It took me a very long time to figure out how you were able to keep killing after you killed yourself, George. It was your anger."

"What do you mean after I killed myself?"

"I'm going to make you remember George."

"Remember what?"

"Everything George."

Glaring at George, Mary took a step toward him. No longer noticing the youngsters deep in each other's arms, his eyes locked on Mary, and George began remembering.

"You were always yelling at me Mary, I remember that."

"Yes, I was George, but why?"

Confusion filled his face, and his eyes grew wide, as he remembered. "It started the day I needed a new thrill and began drinking and whoring around leaving you sitting in our room alone. Wasn't it?"

"Yes, and what finally happened? Why did you do that George?"

"I'd come home and see you in the old threadbare clothes. Our money gone and I couldn't stand it Mary. We were going to have to move back to the old shack and the money I make at the mine we'd barely keep food on the table."

"Weren't we happy there George?"

"Yes, but we were so much younger Mary. I wasn't old and bent. I got so angry, looking at you in that threadbare gown."

"And then what?"

George Haint

"Panicking, George whispered. "I kept getting angrier."

"And....?"

"I, I, I..."

"Remember." she murmured."
"I picked up the cheese knife and slashed your face, didn't I?' He muttered. 'I killed you after that didn't I Mary? There was so much blood, it was everywhere. All I could see was the blood, and you lying in it."

"Yes, George. But remember the rest."

"It felt like I'd killed myself, Mary."

"You did George. You plunged that knife right into your heart. But your anger only grew from your remorse. It gave you the ability to shut out what you had done, come back up here and learn how to move and kill as a ghost. That's why no one could ever find the whore killer. You are dead George."

"Oh, dear God, Mary what have I done?" He said sinking to the floor, face in his hands sobbing.

"You could never remember who was your first. It was me. And now it's going to stop."

"NO, it couldn't have been you. I always loved you, Mary, I still do."

"And I love you, George but can't unless you face up to yourself and let go of the anger, neither of us can move on."

She sunk to the floor next to her sobbing husband, and put her ghostly arms around him, holding him tightly as he continued to cry. Horrified with who he had become, George was finally facing himself. What would happen next was anyone's guess. But Mary would not allow him to kill again.

Sound asleep on the dusty bed, the young couple slept deeply, lust satisfied. At least for now.

Several prostitutes were killed in the Virginia City area during the eighteen hundreds, including the most famous one Julia Boulette who was known to have a heart of gold. None of the murders were ever discovered.

This photo of an old miner's shack was taken between Carson City and Virginia City between the Silver Hill and Gold Hill area by Helen Diessner, who told me it gave her the idea for this story.

This is the only story to my knowledge that my sister ever wrote. I hope she likes the way I wrote the middle to the end she wanted.

One of the herds of the wild horses that came down from the hills behind her apartment. When I stayed at her apartment, I too loved to watch them. Sometimes they'd make their way down through the parking lot of her building, stopping traffic when they wished to cross the road.

Another herd that could be seen along the road between Carson City and Virginia City.

Helen feeding a squirrel a carrot in her later years before COVID.

Bucket of Blood Saloon where for a time she bartended.

The Way it Was Museum where she worked for many years.

Virginia City Nevada is one of the most haunted places in the country. Some places the public is not allowed into because of the hauntings.

www.ingramcontent.com/pod-product-compliance
Lightning Source LLC
Chambersburg PA
CBHW071226130626
46555CB00004B/1868